HERO Love

HERO LIFE

By

Pamela Rossiter

Hero Life, Hero Love

iUniverse books may be ordered through booksellers or by contacting:

iUniverse
1663 Liberty Drive
Bloomington, IN 47403
www.iuniverse.com
1-800-Authors (1-800-288-4677)

Because of the dynamic nature of the Internet, any web addresses or links contained in this book may have changed since publication and may no longer be valid. The views expressed in this work are solely those of the author and do not necessarily reflect the views of the publisher, and the publisher hereby disclaims any responsibility for them.

Any people depicted in stock imagery provided by Getty Images are models, and such images are being used for illustrative purposes only.
Certain stock imagery © Getty Images.

ISBN: 978-1-5320-7139-3 (sc)
ISBN: 978-1-5320-7140-9 (e)

Library of Congress Control Number: 2019904249

Print information available on the last page.

iUniverse rev. date: 04/10/2019

HERO LIFE, HERO LOVE

PAMELA ROSSITER

Chapter 1.

Robert Ross was waiting for her granddaughter, it will be a great day. It is her birthday, she is 5 years old now. He bought her a pink bicycle and pink cake. His veteran friends were waiting to give her the gifts they brought. She ran down the stairs and saw lots of balloons and ran to grandpa. Then she saw the bicycle and asked Grandpa "Is that my bicycle?" And he nodded. She said "Are my mommy and daddy and grandma coming to the party?" Grandpa said "They are in all in heaven, looking down on you every day." She replied "If I ride my bike really fast, maybe ii can see them." He knew that she would ask question about her mommy and daddy and grandma. They were all killed in a car crash. His friends each had a gift for her. She got a turtle, a bird, and many other great gifts.

. . .

Grace Ross ran down the steps of the college with her diploma in hand, Grandpa I did it she hugged him. You are the love of my life I am so proud." Well you will never guess what I am going to do with my four million dollars from my Trust fund.

Two years later

Grace stood at the gates with grandpa,, this is the town she said with a smile It took 2 years and four million dollars, this town is for veterans that have nowhere to go, only vets and there family are allowed to live here' She opened the gates, there was a long line outside and no one would be turned down. She greeted each person in line. The court yard was full with people. Grace on the step "Good morning welcome to the Town. I am Grace Ross and this is my grandpa Robert Ross this town is a place for all of you, we believe you are hero's you are here to live a life that you deserve. We have everything you need, a hospital, Gym, Restaurant

T, Schools, Park, Pool, Church, for starters .There was talking, one person asked how much does cost?

Nothing

Chapter 2

I want to tell you about the town, this is Rick Simmons and Jack Strat They are in charge of security .If you have an issue give them a call. We have everything you will need, our hospital has doctors and nurses live here. There are four hundred homes and Apt you can pick where you want to live. Several people hugged her. A little girl grabbed her hand and said "My daddy only has one leg, but he can run really fast." She continued, whispering "He just got a new leg." Annie I am sure Miss Ross has things to do,MS Ross I am Kurt Thomas and my wife Joan We both are grateful to be here. we need help .Could we talk tomorrow after we get settled in our new house., of course they shook hands, I will see you tomorrow I am happy that you are here. As she walked to the hospital several people waved and said good morning she smiled. DR Morton

Stood in the hall way I Hi Grace, Morning, do we have any patients yes we have Twelve at the moment several need help. Do you have gentleman in a wheel chair? We have two. By the way how is grandpa? He is fine he loves to talk to everyone and can't wait for spring, to get the garden planted.

Grace added I believe he has talked to everyone. He is amazing. The stack of papers were on the table, 3 other security guys were looking through to make sure each person was a veteran. Gracie was on the porch of the house, she and grandpa shared. People walking around, she saw a man in a wheelchair and he stopped in front of her, she said good morning. He looked at her, he said where the restaurant, down the sidewalk on the left is. He backed up and said how much does it cost? Everything here doesn't cost anything. She said can I walk with you and introduce you to the chef's? He said have you noticed I don't walk anywhere, I'm sorry why you don't leave me alone as he wheeled to the restaurant. She thought it might be harder than she thought to help people.

Mike was in the courtyard and meeting with all the people here. Most of you have been if anyone has issues. A man that Grace did not know said to her that she was an angel. She looked over her shoulder and saw that most of you had jobs before you joined the military. If any of you want to go back to what you did before you are welcome to do that. Ken raised his hand, "I was a second grade teacher." Grace said, "We need teachers." Another person said they were an accountant, the next one said they were a chef. A lady said she was a gardener, Grace said if any of you want to go back to that I will help you do that . Most of them to be needed .all of you are needed.

Chapter 3

She walked to the Hospital and wished had her coat, it was starting to snow she walked faster. The hospital s windows for all the patients for their safety and the doctors and nurses.

Hi doc I am here to see Scott Allen. Ok but he well not talk to you, he has not said a word since he came here. I know but I will never I give up. She knouted on the door, he was sitting in the wheel chair. Good morning, no response, I know that PTSD and you lost your legs, I wat to help you, but you have to want to get better. Fuck you don't know anything about me. I am here just waiting to die Why do you even care.

Because everyone has a place in this town

Get out.

Ok, see you tomorrow.

Grace looked outside and the snow coming down, she

Ran to the, office Grandpa was talking to a man she had not seen before Grace I want you to meet Sam she shook hands she didn't like him but not sure why, he smiled. Grandpa said lets go outside everyone is having a snow fight. Tim came out with trays of hot chocolate. Laughter made her simile. Sam asked Grace where your coat is. He took his jacket and put on her Shoulders, Thanks, a man was standing behand her Are you C Grace? She turned around Yes I am. I am Zack, Welcome We are having snow party, do you like hot chocolate Grace I am chocolate both laughed I, didn't noticed. He said you are funny, instantly, she liked him.

Sam asked, are you Marine yes, fifteen years and you? Yes Grace tell me about this town.

We have thing you need. We, have a hospital a and Rest aunt, school, church, Basket Ball, Golf, bike trails, and horses, and the best part, 400 homes and Apts. So you should take a walk and pick your house. Just like that? Yes she asked Sam if he had picked a place. Not yet, Zack we should get Grand pa to go with us .Grandpa was happy to help them. Zack said, "Tell me about Grace." Well, she is tiny but she is in charge and always does the right thing. She spent most of her money building the town. But she was determined, and never stopped."

Grace walked over to Zack, "Can I talk to you?"

Mike, Jack

Sam and Grandpa What did do you do before you joined, the military, He said I was a builder contractor She had a big smile, and said, would do me a favor Yes, whatever you need . Jack asked her, do you want me to get Morgan and Jessie? Yes.

Grace said we have two guys that argue and fight. I don't want to

Make them, leave, but we don't allow fighting at the town. Grandpa said maybe Zack time to get settled said I will build anything you want, what do to want me to build? She said a baseball field for. the kids and adults too . And seats for the people.

I would love if Morgan and Jessie could help. You .She looked him and he said When can I start? Grace hugged him. Whenever you want. I don't know how to thank you. I am the one to thank you for letting me to live here and I get to build.

Morgan and Jessie looked at Grace. She said to Mike can you take care of this for me? Will do Thanks.

It had been two weeks, so Grace went to see how Zach was doing. She was surprised to see a group of men, all working. Zach saw her and walked to her. "Hi, Grace; how are you?" Doing great. She asked where did all these guys came from, it seems everyone wants to help. Can I ask you? A question. He said sure can. Why are you limping? When I got my prostates' for my legs they have never been right

He said, not a big deal, She grabbed his hand lets go. Where are we going, to see the doctors? I can't do that, I have to go back to work. She said it won't take long. You are getting new legs.

He said I don't have that of money. You don't need money.

Chapter 4

She woke up early making pancakes for Grand pa, his favorite breakfast .Good morning Grace, Hi Grand pa how are you? I could not be any better I have a lot to do today. Like what? Putting a group of people that want to help with our flower' and vegetable gardens. I have 20 people already, it will be wonderful.

I hope you are not working too much. I am having the time of my life. I want to tell you how proud I am of you. Thank you I could never have done this without you. You know you are my life .He stood up and hugged Grace. See you later I love you.

L Love you too

Chapter 5

The weather was slowly getting warmer. She thought that it would soon be nice and everyone would be able to enjoy it. She did not like the cold, anyway. She looked at her watch and started walking faster. There was too much to do, but she had several things to do and excited about the outcome. On her way to the hospital she noticed GP, Zack and Sam working together in the garden, they waved she could hear laughing .She was so happy that GP had made lots of friends. Everyone at the town knew him, and they all called him Grandpa She said off to the hospital.

Scott's window was across the hall of Teste waved to Scott and he turned around, as she went into Tex's room .She had a view of Scott, he kept turning around, she smiled. Tex asked why are you here? I always visit new people,

I have been here three weeks. And I don't have anything to say to you. I know you are battled with surveil r guilt and I want to help you. I don't want any help I am here to die not to live. Just get out.

S I have a favor to ask you. I have a guy his name is Dean and needs help, if you help him I well stop coming here every day. How long is this going take. Not long. Well if it gets you off my back I will help Ok get your coat now? Yes get going, She opened the door, and walked down the hall, Tex was putting his jacket on a d ran to keep up with her .Were are going not too far,She looked at him when he saw the horses, turned to her. Are three's yours Well they belong to the town, How many do you have? Right now we have fifteen there were two horses in the ring walking toward Tex, he was petting one when a man walked out of the barn, he ran to Grace Hi Dean said do we have a new worker, yes he turned to Tex welcome to my world they shook hands Tom said I love horses Grace smiled. Looking at the horse, he said, she is beautiful. What is her name?" ",Stella." "She doesn't like me and reminds me of my ex-wife." She said, "She didn't like me either." Tex and Grace laughed. She loved that sound because it was Tex .Hey lets go to breakfast and talk, Grace Can you come with us I would love to but I have a lot of work to do maybe next time. He walked to her. Pick her up in his arms and kissed her cheek, you saved my life today, I don't know how to thank you.

, just be happy and make this a new life. No regrets

Chapter 6

She was on her way back to the hospital, she is so excited to talk to Scott, I hope he will be happy, but it could make him angry. Doctor Harmon met at the door, Scott was sitting on the bed, she opened the door good morning Scott. He turned around, Doe s any one here know how to knock on the door. Doc said we are here to talk,

Don't have anything to say,

Someone knocked on the door Grace smiled .Scott yelled come in. Kelly smith the head nurse walked in She handed an envelope to the doctor, Grace, asked is Doctor Adams here yet?

Yes he just came in, are you ready for him yes Scott moved to his wheelchair, Wait is going on here, are you getting rid of me? He looked scared I have no ware to go. The door opened and a tall young man walked in Good. morning

Grace, h I Mark Doc Harmon shook hands, I want you to meet Scott .I am going to let you discuss our plan. Call me when you are done. Scott said please don't leave me. Scott, you are in good hands, everything will be fine, I promise.

Grace was walking up and down the hallway. Scott had been with the doctors for two hours what could they talk about for that long. She just had to find out what, was going on, she didn't' knock on the door she All three guys were laughing and talking football .Scott looked at her and wheeled to her looking in her eyes She couldn't tell if he was happy or mad. Scott said Grace you are a real angel. Do you know that the docs are going to get me legs and I will be out of the chair The, VA said that I would in a chair forever She said they were wrong

Doctor Harmon said, this was Grace that planned all of this, He had tears, and Grace kissed his forehead. OK. Can we get a date to change his life yes I will call both of you tomorrow.

Scott asked how much h does this cost. Zero I feel so bad for the way I treated you. That is said and done and I hope we can be friends .you are amazing Grace.

Doctors moved to the door. We will let you know tomorrow Grace said Thanks.

Grace looked t Scott Can we talk for a minute? I will do anything you want. I don't think I have been so happy I am happy too. She said what did to before you became a solder. I owed a gym, I worked out every day, and helped others to get heathy. I want you to go with me to see something. Ok.

They went inside a building, Scott said where we going, this is the gym, she opened I was the door of the huge gym. Is this your gym? It belongs to everyone, it is beautiful. I think I missed a lot because I was a jerk. I can't wait to see the whole town. You Wii be so surprised. He said, what the signs are for. Inspire to heal and live a happy life. Scott said my favorite e is freedom and home.

She thought today was the best day at the town, but there a lot more people to help. She walked out of the hospital, and Mike was walking toward, her, Hi Grace, how are you doing. ? It has been a great day. How are you? I have five new vets and they are firemen. That. Is great they want to move in today OK can you and Jack take care of that? Of course

How is Maggie doing? He looked I guess embarrass I guess you saw us at the café yes here there are no secrets I think you are a great couple

We have known each other since grade school. Maybe you and Maggie will be the first wedding at the town he looked at her I didn't say anything about marriage, she laughed .You are scared. Well I don't see a ring on your finger. Ok I am scared too. Jack walked to them. Hi Grace I haven't seen you all day, is everything ok yes Could I talk to you for a minute sure Mike started to walkaway Jack said Mike come back I want you to hear this too, Ann and I have something we want to tell you, She had never seen Jack never iOS he was always in charge kind of guy. Did something happen yes well I are you going to tell us, she tuned to mike he shook his head. Ok just tell us and we can help.

Ann and I are going to have two babies, How did this happen. Mike said If you don't' know how this happened you really have a problem Grace started giggle this is wonderful, the Jack said to Mike, you are so funny. Grace said I love babies Sam was standing behind her he said if you marry me we can have lots of babies Mike and Jack said that is a good idea. now all three of you are funny. I have to go. She mumbled to herself, men, can't live with them and can't live without them.

Grace was tired but

At a great day .she stopped at the restaurant to see Tim. Hi

Grace nice to see you how are things going. My new helpers are doing great

I am so happy to hear that. Do you have apple, pie sure It is for grand pa right, yes he loves it. Thanks, see you later.

Chapter 7

Women

She was walking home with the pie, and a few people waved at her. She was so happy. She opened the door to the house where she and grandpa lived. She called out Grandpa are you here, no answer she went in the kitchen and he was laying on the floor, she tried to wake him up. She hit the emergency button, she was on the floor holding his head and crying. She heard someone coming in, she was yelling help when Mike, Jack, and Sam ran in, He won't wake up why won't he wake up, S am said Grace let go so we can see, Mike and Jack picked her up both held her, they all knew he had has passed away The doctors ran in and looked at Grandpa and they knew he was gone. Grace said he is just sleeping. The tears would not stop. Doc Harmon gave her a glass of water and a pill. The sadness affected hit everyone, the doc asked if Grace has family, no one knew, she never talks about herself. Everyone wanted to stay Nick came in with food. .Grace was asleep with Sam holding her. And joined in the conversation I was with him most of the day, he was fine. This is so sad. The death of grandpa spread, like fire. Grace woke up and Sam was still had her in his arms .Grace opened her eyes, Please tell me that I just had a nightmare and Grand Pa is ok. Grace I am sorry. The tears filed her eyes and Sam s eyes were wet, he loved her so much, and wanted to protect her. She said he was my

Everything, and I don't have any family, He said you have me and four hundred people in our town that love you. We are all family. Everyone wants to help in some way. The doorbell rang Sam opened the door, Mike, jack and Tim came in. We have breakfast. Each one of them hugged her. Mike said we all love you and will do anything to help.

Grace said she was not ready to talk to anyone Sam stayed with her, and she needed to get out of the house I am not going out, I think that is what most of the people that came here,he said you are right she pondered and I have to do the right thing, will you come with me one condition what is that give me a kiss she looked in his eyes and something happens that she saw him for the first time, and shocked her how kind he is.

Everyone came to say good bye to Grand Pa

Grace walked to the steps of the courtyard, to speak.

Thank you coming, and Grandpa would love to see how much love our town has.

We all help each other. We are all family, it doesn't matter what color you are or where you came from and if you are a male or female you are al l heroes

Sam was so proud. Of Grace, she is amazing Grace She took Sam's hand and they walked thru the crowd with hugs and shaking hands. Sam thank you .I could not have done that alone.

You make me strong. Sam said I love you.

They got back to the house, she said it seems so quiet and lonely. Sam picked up a piece of paper Grace what it that? Sam said a note from Grandpa.

You should read this ok. She sat at the kitchen table. And opened the note.

Please don't read this until I have pass away.

Grace, if you are reading this I will be in haven, I had a good life and the only thing I regret was when I. was in Vietnam. the things we had to do and see. I never talked about it with you. When you. Came to live with me, I was blessed to start a new life and let go of the bad things. When that happen

I became a very happy man all because of you.

You grew up to be an exteriorly woman, I'm so proud of you and all the things you do to help people and I believe you give them a second chance to be happy and whole.

You are always going to be my angel. .She took a breath and cried, Sam hugged her she saw the tears on Sam's face. Grace I have something to do, and will be back soon. I love you.

Sam can back a couple hours later, he was holding a blanket and, handed it to her. There was a puppy licking her face, Sam said her name is Roxy, she is an English Bull Dog . She is yours. She kissed him and said I love you He asked her, will you marry me? She said maybe.

She walked to Grand Past room She missed him so much and the tears filled her eyes... Even having so many people in the town she felt lonely. Then she thought that he would not want her to be sad. It occurred to her, he would want her to do something that everyone could have fun. I know the perfect thing to do.

Chapter 8

It was a beautiful summer day, all the flowers were in bloom and Grace knew Grandpa would love it. She knew he was in heaven looking down, happily smiling. A group of people saw her. One of them asked "Grace, Do you love the garden?" "Yes, thank all of you for all your hard work."

Her phone rang. Answering it, she heard, "Hello, Grace. I need you at the office right now."

"Jack, I will be there in a minute." She ran, thinking something bad happened .she saw a group of women sounding. Him He waved to her. They all were talking, Grace was trying to get their attrition, so she whistled very loud. Then silence, she said good afternoon ladies

I am Grace Ross How can help you? One women stepped forward. MS Ross' we would love to live here. All of us are widowed all of our husbands are

Veterans
Grace looked at the women, most of them are very young with babies I am so sorry for your loss. I think that we all would be

honored to have all of you. Each women gave Grace a hug. She knew it was the right thing to do. Jack said I will take care of getting them to their new homes. A little boy grabbed her hand, what is your name Jake like my dad, she said that is a great name he said he died and now I am in charge of my family and my mom cries a lot.

Do you have a house for me, and my mom and sister? Yes. I will have to see it to make sure it is ok. Grace saw Sam behind she smiled and said this is Sam and will go with you to look at the house. Sam said nice to meet you Jake, how old are you? I am nine but my birthday is pretty soon and I will be ten .Tomorrow I will check out the town. Grace looked at Sam and whispered, I think you could volunteer to help Jake, he has a lot of worries for a nine year old.

I will gladly take him under wings. She kissed him his cheek. He said do you want to get married? Nope. Jake said hey Sam I am ready to see the house. Mom I will see you later, after I check the place. She watched them walk away and saw Jake take hold of Sam's hand. She knew Sam would be a good thing for Jack and maybe a good father with his own child if he ever gets married. Karen said, "I can't thank you for all things you have done for all of us." Grace said, "You're welcome, Let me know if your home is okay." She laughed, "Jake will let you know."

Will you tell your husband thanks for his time with Jake? Grace said, Sam is not my husband, he is a friend. Karen I am sorry, the way he looks at you like a man in love Grace said I have to go.

Chapter 9

Grace decided what to do in memory for Grandpa.

She asked Mike, Jack Tim, Zach, Scott, Ted, Dean, and Sam to meet in the Court yard. I asked all of you to help me plan a Hugh party for the whole town and celibate Veteran's Day.

I have asked everyone to participate with I Idea of what we want.

I think Grandpa would love the town to celebrate life.

Mike said, I will get flags, Tex and Dean said we can have horse rides for the kids. We have two new ponies. Tim said we can have BBQ and maybe a pie contest and a limeade stand for the kids.

Zach and Scott said we could have a baseball game with the ladies and guys. The field will be done in a couple weeks Zach said thanks to Scott, Morgan and Jessie.

The town was bussing with everyone gritting pies done and Tim ready to start the grille Grace was waiting for Zach and Scott. She turned around, and saw both of them were walking to her. She could not stop the tears, both of them hugging her. She couldn't speak. Scott said we are so grateful that you saved our lives. Zach said you really amazing Grace.

It was Veterans Day, Grace was excited the town was bussing, there we people everywhere with kids waiting to ride the ponies 'tables of. Food, and she heard music, what a great day.

Sam and Jake walked to her, Jake said Hi miss Grace I get to play baseball today, I get a hat with my name on it Wow, and have you ever played baseball? Kind of Sam has teaching me that is good, she turned to Sam and smiled. Morgan and Jessie were walking to her. Hi Grace we want to thank you for all the things you have done for everyone in this town. To day you have given people hope faith, love, trust and everything matters.

After the party it seemed different. In a good way. Sam said I am so proud of you. There is one

Chapter 10

Since the party 'Grace had time to visit the women, she was surprised that Zack was working on the roof of the new library and community center for meetings and parties.

Scott came around the building jogging with several men and women. He waved to Grace, yelled I can run!

She heard the panic siren ringing and ran to the Courtyard. Jack Grace it happened! What happened? I am a father! We have a boy and girl. Is Ann doing ok? She is fine, I am so happy for you. Have you named them? Yes he is Jack and she is Jill that is great. Jack said I am going back to the hospital, do

You and Sam want to go with me, I want you to see the babies. They were beautiful. Sam said do you want to get married and have babies. She didn't say anything

Chapter 11.

It was early as she walked to the rest aunt to see how Tim was doing. He as three new people working for him. He was one of the first people to live in the town, she was grateful to have him here

She opened the door and Scott, Mike, Zach and Tim were having coffee, Good morning. How are you? Good they all answered Hoping for a quiet day.

The alarm t blasted and they all ran to the door and their phones were ringing, Doctor Harman said I need help at the hospital right now.

Grace was the first to get to the hospital, Doctor Harman. The man is in the room next door, he has a gun. She told no one comes in the room no matter what happens. Sam said you are not going in that room .She said back off I know what I am doing.

That is first time she raised her voice to anyone, they were all stunned. She walked in the door and closed it, she walked toward him, and he had the gun pointed at her.

What is your name? Keith, my name is Grace. Silence. She moved closer to him he said are you just stupid, I can shoot you right now, silence again. She said Keith you know you are not a killer.

I think you just need someone to talk to. This town is for people like you.

When was the last time you had something to eat? Tim left go get food, I don't know.

Grace said am going to get some food and water, he said, I don't want any charity. It is not, everything here is free.

I am not hungry, I am just really tired. Ok. Can you give me your gun? NO!

I can't give it to you ok, Can you tell me why. He said a soldier never gives up his weapon. OK. Can we sit down? He said I guess so, she moved chair close to him...

There was a knock on the door. He jumped up and pointed the gun. She stood up, saying "It is just the chef with the food."

Keith said "I told you I am not hungry."

She said "He made it for me."

Keith asked, "Are you hungry?"

Grace replied, "Yes, I am going to open the door and get the tray."

He said, "I will have my gun pointed at you, so don't do anything to make me shoot you."

Tim slid the tray in to the room and closed the door. Grace picked up the tray and walked to the chair. Keith was looking at the food She said do you want to share this with me?

Let's put the tray on the small table, heisted and put the gun on the table behind him.

She said you should try the France toast, he looked at her and said Way are being so nice to me? She said you are not a bad person, you just need help. Do you have a family? They told me to stay away from them, and get help. I know I am a different person after being in

They told me to come to this town. Grace said I am happy you are here, because you are safe and you will get all the help you need.

Keith said nothing is going to help. She said, could you stand up? He said are you going to kick out of here? No, I just need a hug, she put her arms around him and she felt the tears.

The door opened Mike, Zach, Tim and Jack surround him He knew he had people that cares am she walked out and Sam grab her arm Do not ever that again., and Scott said are you crazy

She said I don't know why you are mad, I was doing my job. Sam said you will never put your life in harm's way again She looked at Sam .I will do what I have to help people. Let go of my arm. On the way out of the door she said By the way I will marry you.

Scott looked at Sam did you hear what she said? Yes, and ran out the door

Chapter 12

The town was almost full Grace checked with Keith and he was working at the hospital

Scott took over the gym and loved it, he had most of the town working. Out daily

Becky was so happy to get new legs and she and husband are having a baby.

Tex and Dean are training horses and helps the children that have lost a parent.

She stopped to see Tim and he was in the middle of a class for people that want to learn to cook He had a big smile and said, thank you.

She went to the oak tree, and sat down. Grandpa was buried, there she would talk to him. She hoped he knew about marring Sam.

She saw Sam, with flowers in his hand. Good morning my love, she smiled I can't believe that we are getting married in two weeks I wish we could get married today.

I talked to Jack and he looks tired' he told me has not slept in three day she chucked, I guess having two babies are a handful.

He said promise me we won't have twins when we have kids. Ok I will work on that, she laughed. The siren was blasting and both of them were running to the courtyard.

There were so many people standing around Grace stood on the steps of the courtyard and every one was silent. Mike, Jack, and Zack told her that there were five men that were trying to get in the town. The want to talk to you.

She said who are. I prefer to talk lone. She said that will never happen.

What are you here for?

We want to buy this town. She said it is not for sale and never will be.

He said I want to talk the owner, she smiled ok, She turned around and ever one in the town was standing be hinder. She said, if you are owner this town raise your hand, everyone had their hands up. She said It is time for you to leave and don't come back. The man stood there and Grace I mean now! The left and things went back to normal

Chapter 13

There were three weddings that next week, Mike and Rachel, Tex and Sally, and Sam and Grace. All of the women in the town were excited to help with the flowers, food and trying to keep the brides calm.

Grace had not seen Sam in three days. Her first thought was that maybe he changed his mind about getting married. Karen Are you ok? I guess, not to sure I want to get married he said Sam is a great guy, you are lucky.

The weddings were all at the same time, the bride's r were, stunning and the town filled with happiness. . The parties went on all night.

Grace realize that having a wonderful man and being in love and someone that cares

She was not feeling well and tried to not think about it.

The next morning, she could hardly get out of bed. She waited for Sam to leave and went to the hospital. Doctor Harmon looked at her and said "Tell me what is going on."

"I don't know," She said. "I am tired and don't want to eat anything."

"Okay, we are going to run a couple of tests."

"I don't want Sam to know."

Chapter 14

Seemed ages for the Doctor to come back,

The doctor said Grace, we found out why you are not feeling well. She stooped, is it bad?

I don't think so but you need to tell Sam. He is in the waiting room

Sam was pacing, waiting for an hour as the clock was ticking.

Finally Grace Open the door ran to him, he picked her and hugged. Her Are you ok?

What did the doctor say? She looked in his eyes and said we are pregnant that is wonderful!

He said I hope it is not twins, and smiled, She said no it is not twins it is triplets their all girls

Kelly Kate, and Kylie were always together and every person in the town knew the little girls. Sam was fascinated with the girls they were just like their mom.

They were Curios about his family.

He said grew up on a farm with my grand ma and grandpa.

I loved all the animals. Sometimes I would sneak we them in the house. I thought it was funny, until a goat ate grandma's favorite dress. When I turned eight teen Grandpa got sick, and passed away. Grandma missed him so much she pasted away three weeks later.

That is when I joined the Marines.

Kelly said lets go ask mom about her life.

The girls asked Grace to tell us about

Your family. She did not like to talk about, her family, but the girls were older now to hear the story.

When I was born my mom was in the hospital for two days. The next day my dad, mom and grandma came to take us home. There was an accident, and I was the only survivor.

My grandpa was the only family I had.

He took me to his home and then it became my home.

He hired a nurse to help him take care of me.

When I turned eight grandpa said, well it just you and me

Or lives were happiness and both of us learned many things.

He learned to braid my hair, I learned how to fish.

He taught me how to swim, I taught him how to sew.

I had a great childhood and loved him more than anything. I miss him so much.

But my life is helping others, and I have a wonderful man and three amazing girls.

Katie said, "I am going to have a town like this one."

Kelly said, "I am going to have a bigger town."

Kiley said, "My town will be the best."

Sam took Grace's hand and said, "We are blessed. This town is magical, and I never want to leave. We have the best family right here. Everyone in the town is family.

Printed in the United States
By Bookmasters